Sir Gadabout

Martyn Beardsley

Sir Gadabout

Illustrated by Tony Ross

A Dolphin
Paperback

Published in paperback in 1994
This edition published in 1999
by Orion Children's Books
a division of the Orion Publishing Group Ltd
Orion House
5 Upper St Martin's Lane
London WC2H 9EA
First published in hardback in Great Britain in 1992
by Dent Children's Books

A catalogue record for this book is available
from the British Library.

Printed in Great Britain by
Clays Ltd, St Ives plc

ISBN 1 85881 055 8

To Elizabeth
For all the joy you have brought me

Contents

1

The Court of King Arthur

A long, long time ago, even before television was invented, there lived a knight called Sir Gadabout. This was in the days of the famous King Arthur and his Round Table. It was an exciting and mysterious time to live in, especially for a knight.

In a misty and remote corner of England stood the castle called Camelot, and there King Arthur gathered the best knights in the land to sit at the Round Table. These knights had to be prepared to go out at a moment's notice and fight villains, dragons, people who drop litter – and generally keep the peace.

If you could travel in time and visit Camelot, you would find the gallant King Arthur, tall and brave, much loved and respected. By his side would be the Queen – Guinivere, beautiful, graceful, and a dab hand at woodwork. Around them you would find all the great knights, whose names might seem odd to us now: Sir Lancelot, Sir Gawain, Sir Dorothy (his name seemed odd even then) and Sir Gadabout.

Now, although Sir Gadabout sat at the Round Table with the best of them, he wasn't quite one of the best knights in the land. It has to be said that he was indubitably the Worst Knight in the *World*. In fact, the March edition of the magazine *Knights Illustrated* voted him the "knight most likely to chop his own foot off in a fight".

His armour was held together purely by rust – and anyway, he'd grown out of it by the time he was eleven. His spear was bent and only good for throwing round corners, and his sword was broken in five places and fixed with lots of sticky tape; it wobbled alarmingly in a stiff breeze. His horse, Pegasus, was knock-kneed and about ninety years-old.

King Arthur felt sorry for Sir Gadabout, who was hard-working and polite. That was

probably why the King allowed him to join the otherwise glorious company of the Round Table.

To be honest Sir Gadabout had not performed as many heroic deeds as the other knights. He'd hardly performed any, unless you count the time when he accompanied the fearsome Sir Bors de Ganis on a mission to rescue the fair maid Fiona from the Isles of Iona. Then he got lost in the eerie mists and ended up in Tipton, some three hundred miles from where Sir Bors was having to get on with the rescue all alone.

Sir Gadabout did once get a dear old lady's cat down from a tree. It wasn't stuck, as it happened (but *he* wasn't to know that) and it only took Sir Tristram three hours to get Sir Gadabout back down again . . .

One day at Camelot a tournament was announced. This is where knights gallop towards each other on horseback from opposite ends of a field and try to knock each other off their horses with long spears. People loved to watch jousting, as it was called, and it was a chance for the knights to show how fearless they were.

A field was prepared outside Camelot castle for the great event. Tents were put up, sand-

wiches and those little sausages on sticks were laid on. A row of seats was provided for the King and his important guests. People came from miles around, and soon a large crowd had gathered. It was rather like a football match, with people supporting their favourite sides and cheering or booing. It would certainly have been on "Match of the Day" if television had been invented – but as I've mentioned already, it hadn't.

King Arthur eventually rose from his seat and announced that it was time for the tournament to begin. The crowd grew more excited than ever, and soon all you could hear was a chorus of "Rhubarb, rhubarb, rhubarb".

Suddenly a voice cried out: "Look! here comes Sir Lancelot!"

Sure enough, he entered the arena on his fiery warhorse and the "rhubarb, rhubarb, rhubarb," grew awesomely loud. Sir Lancelot was wearing splendidly polished silver armour that shone and glinted in the sun. Beneath his armour he had curly blond hair and an impressive suntan. He sat up straight in the saddle (even famous knights had to sit up straight) with his squire (a kind of personal servant) trotting beside his horse. The squire

carried Sir Lancelot's spears. It was a glorious sight.

Then came Sir Gadabout – for he was to be Sir Lancelot's opponent.

Sir Gadabout was not in his usual rusty armour, and on the outside he actually looked a fine figure of a fighting man. But on the inside it was a different story.

He had borrowed his brother's armour for this special occasion. The trouble was that Sir Gadabout was considerably smaller than his brother, who was called Sir Felix le Flab. There was so much room inside the suit of armour that when Sir Gadabout got an itch on his knee (which was quite often for some reason) he was easily able to reach down inside and scratch it.

His arms didn't even come near to the end of his armour's arms, and his head barely came half-way up the helmet. The suit was so roomy that he even had his cheese sandwiches (which he was saving till lunch-time) tucked inside the breastplate – the bit that goes round the body like a metal coat. However, it soon became hot inside the armour, and after a short time the cheese began to smell rather strongly.

Trotting proudly alongside Sir Gadabout was Herbert, his loyal squire. He was carrying his master's spears, although Sir Gadabout only had two: the bent one and the one belonging to Sir Felix le Flab which was a bit greasy and tended to slide backwards through his hand rather than knock the opponent off.

Herbert had been with Sir Gadabout for many years and was absolutely devoted to his master. He was a short and stocky young man with thick black hair which came to a fringe almost covering his eyes, rather like an old English sheep-dog. He wasn't very clever, but he had a mighty punch. Few people dared laugh at Sir Gadabout when Herbert was nearby.

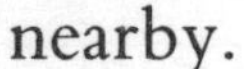

The two knights came to a halt at opposite ends of the grassy arena. The squires gave them each a spear, and the crowd chattered "Rhubarb, rhubarb, rhubarb" expectantly. The two horses pawed the ground impatiently, awaiting the charge.

Then King Arthur rose, produced a red silk handkerchief from his pocket, and waved it in the air. The crowd fell silent, holding its breath in anticipation . . .

King Arthur blew his nose on the red silk handkerchief with a loud "PAAARP" and then started to chat to Guinivere about what was for dinner. The crowd had to start breathing again, since they were beginning to turn blue in the face. Someone nudged King Arthur to remind him that he was supposed to be starting the tournament.

"What? Oh, yes!" He was about to hold up the silk handkerchief again, but just in time he remembered what he'd done with it. He hastily stuffed it into his pocket.

He took a deep breath: "Ladies and gentlemen!"

The crowd held its breath once more. The horses snorted and the knights steeled themselves.

"Let the joust commence!"

·2·

The Joust

A cheer went up! Sir Lancelot dug his spurs into the horse's flanks and the powerful, magnificent beast reared and surged towards Sir Gadabout.

Sir Gadabout also dug his spurs in. His horse kicked out its hind legs in a temper and bumped Sir Gadabout three feet into the air even though his armour stayed firmly in the saddle. When he landed he discovered that he was sitting on his cheese sandwiches. It was too late to do anything about it – Sir Lancelot was pounding down the field and getting closer. The crowd roared.

"Oh, come on!" Sir Gadabout shouted at his horse. Herbert spotted the problem and gave Pegasus a crafty kick in the rear, and off the old horse charged. Sir Gadabout held his large shield tightly and pointed his spear purposefully at Sir Lancelot. He felt the cheese sandwiches squish as he bumped up and down.

Now, Sir Lancelot, being the Greatest Knight Ever, wasn't very worried about jousting with Sir Gadabout, the Worst Knight Ever. Just for fun, he aimed his spear at the side of his opponent's bottom. As they came together with a thundering of hooves, his spear found its target and Sir Gadabout shot into the air with a yelp which made the crowd howl with laughter. But even Sir Lancelot was surprised when, on turning at the end of the field for another charge, he discovered a squashed cheese sandwich hanging from the end of his spear. Furthermore, his horse seemed to have forgotten about the jousting; it was craning its neck and trying to get a bite of the tasty morsel dangling before its eyes. The crowd laughed even louder.

Sir Lancelot wasn't used to being laughed at. He threw the sandwich away angrily and urged his horse on. This time he meant business. The crowed sensed it, and began to whisper "Rhubarb, rhubarb, rhubarb," in a worried way when they thought of what might happen to Sir Gadabout.

The horses bounded towards each other. They went faster and faster. Sir Gadabout's armour clanked louder and louder. In fact, Pegasus was galloping at such a pace that bits began to drop off. First the knee-guards fell off, then a shoulder-piece. Sir Gadabout's body armour began to turn around like a roundabout and ended up back to front.

The speeding knights came together with a fearsome crash and the crowd gasped. Surely someone must have been killed?

First everyone looked at Sir Lancelot, and saw that he was all right. Then they looked at

Sir Gadabout and there were cries of horror – he was headless! Sir Gadabout's helmet rolled on the ground smashed and dented, and for all anyone knew his head was still inside it! There was a stunned silence.

Sir Gadabout's body, with a space on his shoulders where his head should have been, was riding aimlessly around the field. The crowd was still deathly quiet . . . and then two eyes popped up above the body armour!

Sir Gadabout had (very wisely) ducked at the last second, and it was just his empty

helmet which had been smashed by Sir Lancelot's sharp spear. Knights of the Round Table weren't supposed to duck, but then Sir Gadabout did a lot of things that knights of the Round Table weren't supposed to do. Anyway, everyone was relieved to see him alive and well.

By this time Pegasus had had enough. The old horse sat down on the ground and refused to budge. Sir Gadabout talked, begged, shouted and even tweaked its ears; but Pegasus wouldn't move.

So the two knights had to finish the fight on foot. They drew their huge swords and advanced on each other. Sir Gadabout thought he might try to frighten Sir Lancelot. He took up a menacing stance and waved his sword in the air, shouting "HUZZAH!" in a loud voice. Sir Lancelot promptly swished his sword and lopped Sir Gadabout's left ear off.

Poor Sir Gadabout's mouth dropped open as he watched his ear (now glowing red with embarrassment) drop to the ground. A scruffy little dog, which had been sleeping in the sun unconcerned by the jousting, opened one eye and saw the ear hit the ground. Quick as a flash it sprang up and made off with the ear in its mouth.

Sir Gadabout chased it as best he could,

clanking along in what was left of his armour.

"That's my ear! Come back with it."

The crowd laughed and someone shouted "Come 'ear!"

During the chase, more armour fell off: nuts, bolts and elbow-protectors. The dog heard the crowd's laughter and realised he'd done something clever. He turned and ran towards the cheering faces with his tail wagging. Sir Gadabout turned too, but his armour stayed in the same place and he fell over backwards . . . or perhaps it was forwards.

Meanwhile the dog dropped the ear and circled it frantically, barking to make sure it didn't try to escape. He was showing off really, but as he'd never had so many people watching him before perhaps it was excusable.

Eventually Sir Gadabout caught up and snatched his ear back. The dog promptly bit him on the ankle and ran away. Sir Gadabout felt a hand on his shoulder. It was King Arthur.

"Never mind, Gads"

"Pardon?" said Sir Gadabout (King Arthur was talking to the side without an ear).

"I said 'never mind'."

"Pardon?"

This time the King leaned forward and

addressed his remarks to the ear in Sir Gadabout's hand.

"I'll get Merlin the Wizard to stick it back on for you."

"Thank you, my Lord," replied Sir Gadabout, bowing. His other shoulder-protector fell off and caught the king a smarting blow on the shin.

"Hmm, we shall also have to see about getting you some decent armour."

Just then Queen Guinivere arrived and Sir Gadabout immediately began to blush bright red. Guinivere was the most beautiful woman he had ever seen and he always blushed when she looked at him. Sometimes he dreamt of rescuing her from some terrible danger. Even *he* knew that he wasn't the best knight in the world, but for Guinivere he would overcome all obstacles, face any danger, and somehow triumph. Perhaps then people wouldn't laugh at him the way they seemed to now.

"I do hope you're not hurt, Gads," said Guinivere kindly. She never laughed at him, and she had been the only one to ask if he was all right.

"I'm quite well, Your Majesty – er, except a little trouble with my ear."

Guinivere turned to her husband, "Merlin will see to it won't he?"

"Yes, dear."

"Right away?"

"Yes, dear."

He summoned Herbert the squire and told him to take Sir Gadabout to Merlin's cottage without delay.

Little did any of them know that this would be the beginning of an adventure; a quest that would have tested the courage and cunning of the World's Greatest Knight. Quite how the Worst Knight was going to cope was another matter entirely . . .

·3·

Merlin

Sir Gadabout and Herbert left the vast walls of Camelot behind them and followed a path deep into Willow Wood where Merlin's cottage lay. It wasn't far from the castle, but hidden in the shade of the thickly crowded trees and undergrowth it was like being in another world. They stopped outside a rickety garden gate and looked up the garden path to a small, ramshackle old cottage with a thatched roof and crooked chimney.

"That's where Merlin lives," said Herbert.

Sir Gadabout looked at the grimy, dusty windows and wondered nervously what lay behind them. The old wizard kept to himself most of the time and Sir Gadabout had never met him – but he had heard many strange stories . . .

He noticed a sign nailed lopsidedly to the garden gate. It said:

BEWARE OF THE TURTLE

"Strange," muttered Sir Gadabout. Slowly, he opened the gate. It made a loud creaking sound. An owl, disturbed by the noise, suddenly shot out of a tree, circled their heads three times and flew away.

"Come along then," said Sir Gadabout to Herbert.

"W-well . . . I'm not sure if a squire is allowed into a wizard's house, sir . . . "

Sir Gadabout was certainly not going by himself and said jovially, "Oh, it will be quite all right."

They walked down the garden path. Neither could see any sign of the turtle they were supposed to beware of – nor could they imagine how a turtle could be a danger to anyone.

A little gold knob by the side of the door had a sign above it saying "PULL". Sir Gadabout told Herbert to give it a tug. He did, and the knob came away in his hand. The end that had been in the wall was shaped like a hammer, and engraved on it was the word "KNOCK". So Herbert knocked on the door with the hammer.

At that moment there was a rustle of leaves above them, and Sir Gadabout expected to see another owl fly out of the tree. Instead, a large turtle leapt from a branch a full thirty feet from the ground.

It dived right at Herbert, shouting, "GERONIMO!"

The squire ducked, the turtle missed. It landed on its back with a thud and lay whimpering and waving its flippers ineffectually in the air.

Meanwhile the door had opened and they were confronted by a rather portly ginger cat.

"Come in," said the cat. "My master is expecting you."

The cat scowled at the turtle floundering on the lawn.

"Doctor McPherson – back in your tree this instant!"

"All right, all right," the dejected reptile replied.

The ginger cat led the two visitors into a rather dark room cluttered with all kinds of furniture and ornaments.

Merlin the Wizard, the great magician, was sitting at a large wooden table amidst a jumble of weird and wonderful items. There was a bottle of steaming, frothing liquid at his elbow; next to that was a stuffed newt in a glass case. There was a pile of old, leather-bound books in one corner, and various strange scientific instruments lay around them.

Merlin had his chin resting on his clasped hands and was staring intently into a crystal ball. Even seated, you could tell that he was tall. He had the thin, wrinkled face of a very old man, yet in contrast his eyes were a fierce blue and as bright as if they were lit up from the inside. He had long grey hair, which was a bit of a mess, and a long grey beard. Bony wrists and fingers protruded from the voluminous sleeves of his black gown.

"Sit," said Merlin, turning his piercing gaze on them. "Now, Sir Gadabout, let me see if I can put your ear back on."

"But – how did you know?" gasped Sir Gadabout.

"He's a wizard, stupid," said the cat, whose name was Sidney Smith.

"I have been watching the goings-on at Camelot for some time," Merlin explained. "I have a feeling that something is going to happen, something unpleasant, but I can't work out what it is. I'm worried."

"Could it be my master's ear being chopped off?" wondered Herbert.

"No, no, you silly person," snapped Merlin, who had a bit of a temper. "Something much more serious than that." With that he went back to gazing at his crystal ball.

Sir Gadabout began to grow impatient, and tried coughing a few times to remind the wizard that he was still there.

"I thought you'd come about your ear, not your cough," remarked Sidney Smith.

"Mind your own business," warned Herbert, who thought that nobody, least of all a cat, should talk to his master like that.

"My master could turn you into a sweaty sock with a swish of his wand," hissed the ginger cat.

"My master could turn you into a dead cat with a swish of his sword," Herbert retorted.

"My master could make your master's *other* ear drop off. *And* his nose, *and* his eyebrows–" and Sidney Smith continued a long list of things which might be made to drop off Sir Gadabout – it all sounded very unpleasant.

Merlin looked up. "Stop that bickering!"

Sidney Smith went away to sulk under a chair.

"Now," began Merlin. "Let me find that spell to get you sorted out." He picked up a huge old book from the pile in the corner and blew off the dust and cobwebs. The dust flew straight into Sir Gadabout's face.

"Ahhh – TISHOO!"

"Bless you," said Merlin. "Let me find the spell to cure that cold of yours."

"I didn't come about a cold, actually."

"Silly me. A cough, wasn't it?"

"It's my ear."

Merlin rubbed his chin. "Your ear's got a cough?"

It seemed that although Merlin could see into the future he wasn't so good at remembering what had happened a few minutes ago.

When things had finally been sorted out, Merlin came across the appropriate spell in his book.

"Here we are: 'Ears – How to wash them, remove things stuck in them, stick them back on again'."

Sir Gadabout was relieved. He was beginning to think he would have to carry his ear around in his pocket for the rest of his life.

"There are two spells," said Merlin. "The Strong Sticking Spell for brave knights, and the Not-So-Strong Sticking Spell for cowards."

"My master's no coward!" Herbert declared.

A cat-like voice from under the chair said, "Bet he is!"

"The Strong Sticking Spell," continued Merlin, reading from the book. "It says: 'First, the knight must pull out a dragon's tooth with a pair of tweezers and bring it back to the wizard'."

Sir Gadabout gulped. There was a cat-like snigger from under the chair.

"Next, it says: 'Tickle a tiger's tummy three times, pull out one of its whiskers and take it back to the wizard'."

There was a sound like someone knocking at the door, but it was just Sir Gadabout's knees knocking. Very loud and very rude cat-like laughter came from under the chair.

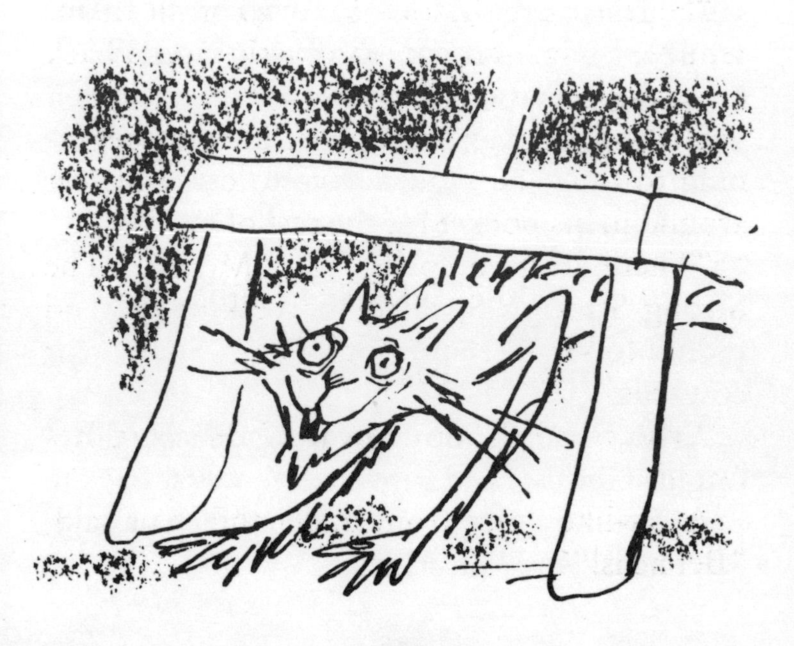

"Are you quite sure about that?" Sir Gadabout asked in a strained whisper.

"It does seem rather odd, I must say," Merlin replied. "It's written in a different sort of writing to the rest of the book – and where it says 'Jump from a tree and land on your nose' there is what looks to me remarkably like a cat's paw-print in the same coloured ink . . ."

The cat-like sniggering from under the chair suddenly ceased and was replaced by a cat-like gulp.

Merlin's face grew dark with anger.

"SIDNEY SMITH!" he roared. "I'll deal with you later. Now I can see the real spell. It says: 'The ear should be held in its proper place while the wizard recites the magic words'."

So Sir Gadabout held his ear in what felt like the right place while Merlin read out the spell:

"Ears are for listening
Don't poke, tweak or grab
Say these words carefully,
And stick back the tab."

At that very moment Sir Gadabout felt a tingle in the ear, and sure enough it was back in place.

"Thank you!" he cried.

"You are welcome."

Sidney Smith emerged from under the chair to have a look.

"It's in the wrong place," he remarked smugly.

"It is *not*!" Herbert protested.

"It – it does feel slightly different to the other one . . ." admitted Sir Gadabout.

"Ha!" exclaimed the cat. "It's lower down and sticking out more!"

Herbert took a good look at both ears. "Hmph. Only a bit . . ."

"As long as it's back on and working," said Merlin.

"'ear, 'ear," agreed Sir Gadabout, who wasn't very good at making jokes – but then what would you expect of the Worst Knight in the world?

·4·

Kidnapped!

Merlin accompanied Sir Gadabout and Herbert back to Camelot, so that he could discuss with King Arthur the worrying things he had seen in his crystal ball. Merlin didn't ride a horse, but despite his great age, the tall, thin wizard swept along, his black cloak flapping behind, and had no trouble keeping up. Sidney Smith scampered along beside his master, occasionally darting after birds and other small creatures foolish enough to cross his path.

When they arrived at the castle, even Sir Gadabout noticed that it was strangely empty. "Something seems different about the place . . . " he mused.

"Where is everybody?" asked Merlin.

"There were dozens of knights here when we left," said Herbert.

"Let's see if we can find the King," suggested Sir Gadabout. One of the knightly things he wasn't so good at was getting down from his horse. As he leaned to one side, about to swing his leg over the horse's back, the saddle suddenly slipped and he found himself hanging upside down from Pegasus' belly.

"What a fool!" cried Sidney Smith.

"Come with me," said Merlin. "This looks serious."

They found King Arthur in the Great Hall of Camelot. It was a vast room, with colourful tapestries hanging from the walls and the Round Table, large enough to seat over a hundred knights, in the centre.

But the Great Hall was empty except for two sad and solitary figures seated side by side at the Round Table.

"Woe is me!" wailed King Arthur.

"The Queen is gone!" lamented Sir Lancelot.

"What a fool I've been," Merlin admonished himself. "I should have guessed."

"I – I don't quite follow," said Sir Gadabout. "The Queen has gone where?"

"She's been kidnapped, you nutty knight," snapped Sidney Smith, who had been with Merlin long enough to tell what his master was thinking.

"Oh, dear!" said Sir Gadabout. "Have all the other knights gone to rescue her?"

King Arthur shook his head sadly and told them what had happened. "Sir Lancelot has just arrived back – he was out slaying an evil giant before breakfast. He wasn't here when the old woman arrived at the castle gates. She said that a herd of fire-breathing dragons had surrounded her cottage and were trying to kill her family. I immediately sent out all of my knights, since it sounded like a big job. She said it was a day's ride to the north. When I came back from seeing the knights off, Guinivere was gone!"

"But didn't you see her go? There's only one way out of Camelot," said Sir Gadabout.

King Arthur shook his head dejectedly.

"Just as I thought," said Merlin. "This is no ordinary kidnap. Someone has been working wicked spells here. You must send out your remaining knights to look for her."

"Surely you don't mean *him*?" Sidney Smith exclaimed in disbelief, pointing at Sir Gadabout.

"I can manage quite well on my own," said Sir Lancelot rather snootily.

"You must both go," said Merlin. "She could be anywhere. Sir Lancelot can go one way, Sir Gadabout and Herbert another. And I'm sending Sidney Smith to help them."

The cat groaned and put his paws to his head.

"Why the cat?" asked Herbert indignantly.

"Because . . ." began Merlin hesitantly. He didn't have the heart to say it was because Sir Gadabout was the Worst Knight in the World.

Sidney Smith, however, did have the heart. "It's because he's useless!"

"Be quiet, Smith," commanded Merlin.

"Well, it's true – he's rubbish!"

"I know I'm not the best of knights . . . " began Sir Gadabout, not being put off by Sidney Smith scoffing, "The *worst*!"

"I shall do my very best to rescue Queen Guinivere. I shall risk my life without a second thought for one who has been so kind to me."

"Thank you, Sir Gadabout," said King Arthur, a tear in his eye.

Merlin drew Sir Gadabout and Herbert aside and spoke again.

"There is another way I intend to help you.

You will doubtless be facing enemies with magical powers, so your – er – skills as a knight may not be quite enough. You could do with a trick up your sleeve, and therefore I am going to make Herbert invisible!"

"Ooer!" said Herbert, and he went so pale that Sir Gadabout, glancing at his squire, thought that it was happening already.

Merlin instructed Herbert to climb on to the Round Table and stand right in the middle. Then he raised his bony arms so that the baggy

sleeves of his black cloak spread out like a crow's wings. "This is a very difficult spell – here we go."

He proceeded to chant strange words in a deep, slow voice: "Beth, Aleph, Cheth, Yod . . ."

Herbert trembled as he stood in the shadow of the tall wizard. He kept looking down at himself to make sure he was still there.

Suddenly, Merlin clapped his hands together and shouted: "BEGONE!"

Herbert's left leg vanished and he promptly fell over.

"Hmm," said Merlin, stroking his beard. "This may take longer than I thought."

However, at the very next attempt he managed to make Herbert well and truly invisible.

"W–when will this wear off?" asked a frightened voice from nowhere.

"It won't wear off. But I can remove the spell when you return . . . I think."

"Where should they start looking?" King Arthur asked Merlin. The wizard delved into his deep pockets and produced his crystal ball. He sat at the Round Table and gazed intently into the luminescent crystal in the palm of his hand.

After several minutes of deep concentration the great wizard spoke in a quiet, faraway voice: "I see a bridge . . . then a little cottage. It's a red cottage with a tall chimney . . . "

He let out a long breath and put the ball away.

"That is the best I can do. I suggest Sir Lancelot turns left out of Camelot and Sir Gadabout right. Look for the bridge and the red cottage with the tall chimney. The best of luck to you!"

And so, the gallant knights rode away from Camelot – Sir Lancelot going left, Sir Gadabout, Herbert and Sidney Smith taking the right-hand path.

Their quest had begun.

·5·

The Mysterious Cottage

Sir Gadabout rode Pegasus; Herbert was on his own pony with Sidney Smith riding inside the saddlebag. Herbert knew a path which led to the river Smidgin, and since no one had any better ideas they decided to try it.

By the middle of the afternoon they found the river, and a man in a boat gave them directions to the only bridge that spanned the foaming waters.

When they arrived at the bridge they saw a sight that made them shudder. A huge knight stood in the middle of the bridge. He was clad in black armour, and wielded a sword that would take two ordinary sized men just to lift it. His feet were planted firm and wide, leaving no room to pass.

Sir Gadabout gulped so loudly that a flock of starlings flapped noisily out of a nearby tree. Herbert clenched his hands into large fists, ready to fight for his master. Sidney Smith ducked into the saddlebag, and they could hear him whistling "Waltzing Matilda" to keep his spirits up.

"Proceed no further," the knight's deep voice boomed out so deafeningly loud that the ground trembled under them.

"He'll cut you up a treat!" sniggered Sidney Smith from inside the saddlebag.

"Quiet, fishface," warned Herbert.

"Er, we'd quite like to come across if it's all the same with you," ventured Sir Gadabout.

"No man shall cross!" bellowed the knight.

"Oh, get on with it, Gads. We haven't got time to waste," cried Sidney Smith impatiently. "Merlin would have turned him into a radish by now."

The Guardian of the Bridge, as he was known, obviously heard this remark.

"That cat will make a nice supper," he hissed in a voice that made the leaves fall off the trees.

"Well said," agreed Herbert.

"Who said that?" asked the Guardian of the Bridge.

"Me, of course," replied Herbert invisibly.

"You?" the Guardian of the Bridge asked Herbert's seemingly riderless horse.

"Yes!" replied Herbert, thinking that the Guardian of the Bridge was looking at him.

The Guardian of the Bridge scratched his head, or rather his helmet.

"Talking horses or not – no one crosses this bridge. I am Sir Pas le Port, and I shall slay anyone who tries."

Sir Gadabout stuck out his chest. "Now look here, my man. I have been sent by King Arthur–"

"BAH!" cried the huge black knight with a shout that blew away rain-clouds which had been gathering overhead. "I was guarding this bridge when King Arthur was still in nappies!"

"What for?" Sidney Smith had popped up.

"What for?" Sir Pas le Port sneered. "WHAT FOR?" he roared, making the bridge shake till it almost collapsed.

"Yes – what for?"

"I've been guarding this bridge since anyone can remember. The reason is obvious. The reason – the reason is this: It's because – well, firstly . . . and then there's . . . Nobody's ever asked that before. It must be because – No, that's not it . . ."

"He's forgotten!" said Sidney Smith.

"Have you?" asked Sir Gadabout.

"NO!" thundered Sir Pas le Port, then, "Well, now you come to mention it . . ."

"Then may we cross?"

"I – I suppose so . . ." he said sounding confused.

They hurried across before he changed his mind.

Just as they were setting off into the forest on the other side, Sir Pas le Port called after them, "Hang on! What am I going to do now? I've been guarding this bridge all my life."

"I know what you can do," said Sidney Smith.

"Please tell me," begged Sir Pas le Port.

"Carry on guarding the bridge."

"But what for?"

"Why, to stop people getting to the other side, of course!" said the cat with a wink. And they hurried away with shouts of "Come back!" from the outwitted knight ringing in their ears.

Before long they arrived at the little red cottage that Merlin had spoken of. When they saw the tall chimney they knew they were on

the right track. They dismounted, and Sir Gadabout went and knocked on the door.

"Clear off!" cackled a voice from inside.

"Oh, dear," said Sir Gadabout. He hated to cause a scene but he sensed that the cottage might be important to their search. The beautiful Guinivere's life was at stake so no stone could be left unturned. He knocked again. This time a little upstairs window flew open.

"Ah!" said Sir Gadabout. "I was wondering if–"

Suddenly a bucket was thrust out of the window and its contents were tipped onto his head. It was a horrible green, slimy, smelly mixture full of little wriggling things. Sir Gadabout, who had removed his helmet, got the disgusting stuff in his ears, up his nose and down his neck.

"Pooh!" gasped Sidney Smith, holding his nose.

Herbert tried to hold his nose – but with it being invisible he couldn't seem to find it. Evil laughter came from the window.

"Old lady," spluttered Sir Gadabout, "do not be alarmed. We only wish to talk to you." A loaf of mouldy bread flew out of the window and hit him on the head.

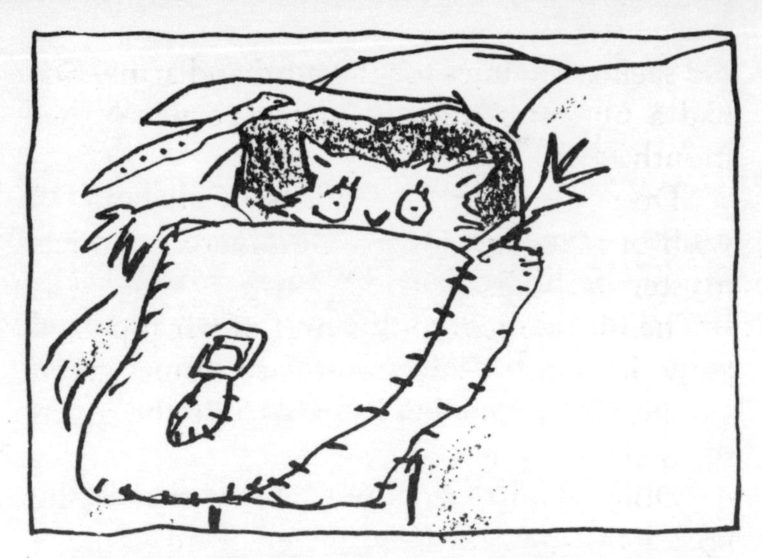

"Good shot!" cheered Sidney Smith. Herbert's invisible hand pushed the cat's head down and fastened the saddlebag.

"Be off with you!" cried the menacing voice, "Or I'll pull the hairs on the back of your neck out. I'll pull your teeth out and bite your nose with 'em. I'll tie your legs in knots. I'll–"

"Leave this to me, sir," Herbert announced suddenly. He had noticed a downstairs window open. He slipped invisibly inside and quickly unlocked the door, letting his master in.

The old woman rushed downstairs.

"EEK! How did you get in?"

She was small and thin, with long straggly grey hair and a ragged dress that looked like an old sack with holes for the head and arms. She had a pipe sticking out of the corner of her mouth.

"Do not be alarmed," said Sir Gadabout. "I wish only to find Queen Guinivere, who has mysteriously disappeared."

The old woman took a puff of her pipe and blew into Sir Gadabout's face some green smoke which smelled horribly like the green slime she'd poured on him earlier.

"Don't know anything about that," she muttered, and puffed out some more smoke – this time, without realising it, into Herbert's face. He started to cough.

"EEK! Who's that?" shrieked the old crone.

"Er, it was me," said Sir Gadabout. "I've got this unusual cough which sounds like it's

coming from somewhere else. I caught it off a ventriloquist."

At that moment a girl came into the room. She had bare feet which were dirty and sore, and she wore a ragged, shabby dress. But the most unusual thing about her was that she wore a paper bag over her head.

"I've fixed the microwave," she said in an unhappy voice.

"Fixed the what?" queried Sir Gadabout.

"Never you mind," hissed the old woman. She turned to the girl, "Be off with you. I told you never to show yourself when I've got visitors."

"Why does she wear that bag over her head?" asked Sir Gadabout.

"Because she's extremely ugly and she'd frighten folks to death without it."

When the girl had gone, Sir Gadabout thought he could hear her crying in the other room. Her miserable appearance had been bad enough, but he was relieved that the paper bag hadn't come off in case the sight of her had turned him to stone.

"Now be off with you!"

"Not until you tell us what you know about Guinivere," said Sir Gadabout firmly. "I'm sure you're hiding something."

"I'm not hiding anything," said the old woman with a mysterious smile. "But the answer is hidden – hidden within walls that run for hundreds of miles. They'll show you a clean pair of heels!"

She shoved Sir Gadabout out of the door, laughing wickedly.

·6·

Castle on the Run

"Walls that run for hundreds of miles," said Sir Gadabout thoughtfully as they rode away. "Camelot's got the longest walls that I know of – but they're not *that* long."

"What about the Great Wall of China?" suggested Herbert.

"Of course!" exclaimed Sir Gadabout. "Off we go!"

"Don't be daft!" said Sidney Smith. "It would take months to get to China and Guinivere's only been gone a day."

"Oh," replied Sir Gadabout and Herbert, looking crestfallen.

Soon the days began to seem like months as they went from castle to castle and town to town looking for walls hundreds of miles long. All the time their hearts grew heavier, wondering whether Guinivere was still safe.

One day they rode to the top of a steep hill to get a good view of the countryside around them.

"Nothing," sighed Sir Gadabout. "Just another castle on top of that hill ahead of us."

"It's on the side of the hill, actually," said Herbert.

"No," said Sidney Smith, "it's at the bottom."

"It's moving!" they all said together.

"After it!" cried Sidney Smith.

He seemed to know what he was doing, so they charged down the hill and galloped across the valley towards the castle, which was now moving quickly. On the way Sidney Smith

made them stop and talk to a farmer ploughing his field.

"What's the name of that castle?" he asked the farmer.

"That? Why, that's Springheel Castle."

"That's it!" said Sidney Smith. "The old woman said 'walls that run for hundreds of miles'!"

"Er," pondered Sir Gadabout as he watched Springheel Castle trotting along a river bank.

"And," added Herbert, "she said it would show us a clean pair of heels!"

The penny dropped. "Spring Heel Castle!" gasped Sir Gadabout. "I just *knew* it. Follow me!"

After a quick spurt they soon caught up with the extraordinary castle. It had stopped at a bend in the river.

Now that they were closer, they could see that it stood on legs. Not wooden legs, nor stone nor metal, but real legs with knobbly knees and hairy shins; one at each corner, and a hundred times bigger than human legs.

"Let's go, sir," said Herbert.

"Wait," said Sir Gadabout. "We don't want to scare it away. You go first – it can't see you. See if you can get us permission to enter."

Herbert walked invisibly up to the castle gates. "Er, excuse me . . ."

Two sentries stood in towers above the drawbridge. One was very fat and the other very thin.

"Excuse who?" asked the fat sentry.

"Me. I'm with Sir Gadabout and we're trying to rescue the Queen. Er, I'm invisible, by the way. Can we come in?"

"Invisible?" said the fat sentry. "I can't just go letting invisible people in."

"It's very important," Herbert pleaded.

"We could see what it says in the rules," suggested the thin sentry.

"That's all very well – but I've never heard of a rule for invisible people!"

Nevertheless he took a little black rule book out of his pocket. "Invisible . . . invisible. It says 'Invisible visitors may only be allowed in on weekdays or at weekends, unless they are Dutch or Turkish, in which case –"

"I'm English!" cried Herbert. So the sentries had little option but to admit Sir Gadabout, Herbert and Sidney Smith into Springheel Castle.

As they walked past, the thin sentry whispered a word of warning in Sir Gadabout's ear. The owner had been put under a spell which made him say the opposite of what he really meant – or at least that's what they thought.

"Oh dear," said Sir Gadabout. "This might prove to be difficult."

The owner of Springheel Castle rushed up and shook their hands (and paw).

"Goodbye!" he announced cheerfully. "I'm not very pleased to meet you."

He was tall, thin and bald, and he wore red and white striped pyjamas.

"I suppose he wears his ordinary clothes in bed," whispered Sidney Smith.

"The Queen hasn't been kidnapped and you don't want to save her. Am I wrong?"

"Yes," said Sir Gadabout.

"No," said Herbert.

"Get on with it," hissed Sidney Smith.

"I can't help you," said the owner. "But first, I don't want you to help me."

"Er . . . oh?" said Sir Gadabout, who was a little lost by now.

"My name isn't Sir Bartholemew the Mistaken. This silly spell wasn't cast on me by the very witch who came this way with Guinivere! If you don't help me, I'll tell you where they didn't go."

After Sidney Smith had explained to his human companions what Sir Bartholemew the Mistaken was talking about, they said to the cat, "Can't you do anything about the spell? You live with a wizard – haven't you learned any magic?"

The cat gave a conceited smile, "I just happen to have a trick or two up my sleeve."

Waving his tail in strange little patterns, he said to Sir Bartholemew:

"Unravel the deeds of one uncouth
Open your mouth and speak the truth!"

As a test to see if the spell had worked, Sir Gadabout asked him if his name was Sir Bartholemew the Mistaken.

"No, it isn't," said Sir Bartholemew.

"It didn't work, you mangey moggy," accused Herbert.

"You are wrong!" declared Sir Bartholemew. "My name *was* Sir Bartholemew the Mistaken. You have cured me of this wretched spell which has made my life a misery, and now I am Sir Bartholemew the True! And true to my word, I shall help you find the Queen and the evil witch who cast this spell on me."

"Oh, do tell us what we should do," Sir Gadabout implored him.

"Ten miles to the north of here," began Sir Bartholemew, "you will find the caves at Crow Hill. The witch who has Guinivere is called Morag, and she has a sister named Demelza who hides in the caves. Morag took Guinivere there, where they're plotting to do away with her unless King Arthur agrees to marry one of them and send Guinivere to live in Venezuela."

"Then we must go at once," said Sir Gadabout.

"You must," agreed Sir Bartholemew the True. "But beware – the old caves are full of danger – and Demelza is as cunning a witch as ever there was . . .

·7·

The Caves of Crow Hill

The road to the North did indeed lead in the right direction, just as Sir Bartholemew had said. It took them most of the afternoon to reach their destination, but just as evening was approaching they saw ahead of them many gloomy, uninviting holes in a steep hillside. These were the Caves of Crow Hill.

As they got closer they could see someone standing in front of the caves. A little man in a blue uniform and peaked cap was standing beside a sign:

CAVES OF CROW HILL

KNIGHTS OF THE ROUND TABLE – £3
CATS – £2
SQUIRES – £1

"Good afternoon, my man," said Sir Gadabout. "My name is Sir Gadabout and I am a knight of the Round Table. We should like to go into the Old Caves."

"Very good, sir. Five pounds, if you please, sir," said the man in a very self-important voice. He would, of course, have charged Herbert as well if he'd been able to see him.

"Oh, dear," said Sir Gadabout in dismay. "I haven't any money. Have you?" he asked Herbert.

The man in the blue uniform took a step back. "Talking to horses!" he muttered to himself. "Keep calm. Don't say anything that might upset him . . ."

Herbert maintained a guilty silence, and Sir Gadabout turned to Sidney Smith. "I don't suppose you've got any money, either?"

"Blimey," whispered the man in the blue uniform. "Talking to the cat, now! This man is not quite right in the head – better let him in before he turns nasty."

He saluted Sir Gadabout. "I do beg your pardon, Mr Gadabout. My mistake – Thursdays are free. In you go!"

Sir Gadabout smiled with relief. "Thank you very much. But can you tell me which cave the witch lives in?"

Demelza, who lived in the deepest, darkest cave, had told the man that she was an eminent archaeologist. In any case he didn't believe in witches.

Nevertheless he thought it best to keep Sir Gadabout happy. "Witch, sir? Why, there's all sorts of them in there."

"Oh . . . but we are looking for one called Demelza."

"Ooh, horrible witch, that one, sir. In the cave by the mulberry bush, Mr Gadabout. Off you go – mind your head." He ushered them in the direction of Demelza's cave as quickly as he could.

It was murky and damp inside. Water dripped from the ceiling, and on the ground

there were stones to stumble on and puddles to step into. Every now and then they thought they could feel wings brushing their faces as if bats were flying around their heads.

Only Sidney Smith was quite at home in the dark.

"Follow me, men," he said jauntily. He led them up and down, round and round, until, in the distance, they saw a light shining from a little room just off the main passageway. Inside there was a woman with long black hair; she was on her hands and knees, digging with a little trowel. Beside her was a small pile of brooches, jewellery and coins.

"I recognise that jewellery," whispered Sir Gadabout. "It belongs to Guinivere!"

They dashed inside at once.

The woman jumped to her feet.

"How do you do," she said, and shook Sir Gadabout's hand. "I'm Demelza Broomspell, the eminent professor of archaeology."

"You're a witch!" hissed Sidney Smith.

"My dear cat," laughed Demelza, "I am one of the country's leading archaeologists, and don't forget it."

"Witch," said the cat adamantly.

"If you call me a witch again I'll turn you into a squid!"

"Ah-HA!" cried Sidney Smith.

"Bah," grumbled Demelza. "What if I am a witch?"

"You must tell us what you've done with Queen Guinivere," Sir Gadabout declared grandly. "Otherwise . . ." and he drew his sword out with a great flourish. The blade hit the low ceiling of the cave and it snapped in two. The broken half cracked Sir Gadabout on the head, knocking him to the floor in a daze.

"I forgot to introduce you to Sir Gadabout," said Sidney Smith. "The Worst Knight in the World."

"Charmed, I'm sure," Demelza said to Sir Gadabout, whose eyes felt as if they were spinning round in different directions.

"I am Merlin's cat," said Sidney Smith. "If you don't tell us how to find Guinivere, I shall cast a spell to turn you into a pleasant old lady, always kind and helpful to people."

Demelza screamed with fear.

"How do I know you can do it? You could be any old ginger tom."

Sidney Smith gave her an icy stare.

"I see I shall have to demonstrate my powers by making you rise in the air!" He could perform neither spell, but was hoping that Herbert was paying attention. He uttered some magic words, making them up as he went along:

> "Bakewell tart
> And lemon sherbert
> Make her rise
> By the power of Herbert!"

Herbert *was* paying attention.

He lifted Demelza off the ground and swung her round and round until she shouted dizzily, "Stop! Stop! I believe you!"

"Right," said Sidney Smith. "Spill the beans."

"Guinivere," said Demelza, puffing and panting from her ordeal, "is with my sister Morag. Our spies told us you were coming here so Morag took her to – to a secret place."

Sidney Smith gave her another one of his icy stares and began to waggle his tail. This frightened Demelza so much that he didn't even have to ask "where?"

"Morag lives in a little red cottage, near a bridge. You can't miss it, because its got a very tall chimney–"

"Oh, no," miaowed the cat. "What fools we were to follow gormless Gadabout all over the place. She was at the very first place we visited! Back to the horses, quickly."

"What day is it?" enquired Sir Gadabout as they helped him to his feet.

·8·

The Crooked Spear

Sir Gadabout, Herbert and Sidney Smith made haste to the cottage where they had encountered the old woman who smoked a pipe and threw things at them. They spurred their horses on as fast as they dared, realising that the old woman was none other than Morag. They were afraid of what she might do to Guinivere if she guessed they were on to her.

Sir Gadabout now realised that the miserable wretch of a servant girl, whom he had been afraid to look at lest her ugliness turn him to stone, was in fact Guinivere.

Old Pegasus led the way and, after the fastest gallop he'd ever made in his life, the red cottage came into view at the end of the forest path.

They were just about to charge up and break the door down when Sidney Smith called, "Wait!"

He had been keeping a look-out with his extra sharp eyes.

"What is it?" asked Sir Gadabout.

"Someone's coming out of the cottage."

Quickly they hid behind a large bush and watched.

Out came the servant girl, all in rags, with the paper bag still over her head. She was accompanied by a rustling mass of branches and leaves.

"Is that a crab-apple tree?" Sir Gadabout wondered out loud.

Herbert thought that his master must still be suffering from the blow to his head, but Sidney Smith, for once, backed Sir Gadabout.

"It is a crab-apple tree."

It loped along on its long roots, keeping a few paces ahead of the servant girl.

"It must be Morag in disguise," whispered Sir Gadabout. "She's trying to make a get-away – and my sword's broken."

"What about your spear, sir?" suggested Herbert.

"The bent one?"

"Yes. You could throw it round the corner whilst we're still hiding behind the bush!"

"You are not throwing that weapon when there are innocent bystanders like me within a three mile radius," argued Sidney Smith.

Sir Gadabout set his jaw determinedly. "I *can* do it! I've had that spear for years and I know exactly how to throw it. Herbert – fetch me my spear!"

Sidney Smith put his paws over his eyes.

"I can't watch."

Sir Gadabout braced himself, waiting for the crab-apple tree to get closer. He was poised with the spear above his head, arm tensed, ready to throw.

Under his breath he counted, "One . . . two . . . THREE," and he hurled the spear with all his might.

It whooshed round the corner, heading for the shambling tree. It whizzed in a circle

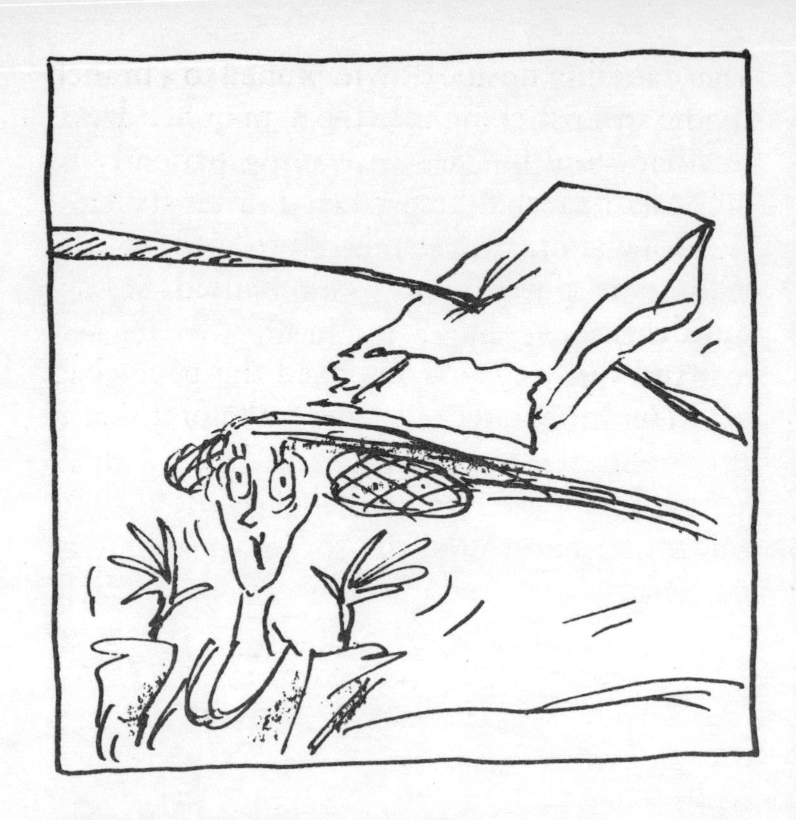

around the tree and headed straight for the unfortunate servant girl. The flashing blade whistled past her head so close that it tore off the bag and revealed Guinivere – much to the amazement of Herbert and Sidney Smith. Then the spear circled upwards and disappeared into the branches of a real tree towering above them. There followed much rustling of leaves and ear-splitting screeches. The next thing they knew, Morag could be seen dangling upside down, pinned to a branch by the spear sticking into the hem of her dress. She had been in the tree waiting patiently to ambush the lot of them when disaster struck.

"Good shot, sir," said Herbert, clapping.

"It was pure fluke," commented Sidney Smith acidly.

"And the way you knocked the paper bag off! You must have suspected all along that it was Guinivere."

"Let's just say," replied Sir Gadabout nonchalantly, "that I noticed there was something

regal in the way she bore herself. I guessed that she must be more than an ugly servant." He coughed a little awkwardly.

"If you believe that, you'll believe anything," said Sidney Smith.

Sir Gadabout scratched his head as he watched the panic-stricken crab-apple tree hopping wildly all over the place.

"But if that's not Morag, who is it?"

"It's me!" cried the voice of Sir Lancelot from its tangled branches.

"Sir Lancelot?" they all exclaimed in chorus.

"Of course," the Great Knight said, trying to retain his composure and failing dismally. "I

was attempting to rescue Guinivere . . . and you interfered."

"Oh dear," said Sir Gadabout.

He was too kind even to think of laughing, but Herbert and Sidney Smith had to go behind a bush until their giggles had subsided.

Guinivere, meanwhile, rushed up to Sir Gadabout.

"My hero!" she cried, and gave him a big kiss, causing him to blush redder than a tomato.

The return journey to Camelot was a jolly one. They even managed to avoid the Guardian of the Bridge; they got a lift across the river from the man in the boat whom they'd met at the start of their quest.

When the little party arrived at Camelot with Guinivere safe and sound the celebrations went on for days.

If you could have been there you might have heard Sir Lancelot telling people, "You see, I allowed Morag to turn me into a tree – a mighty oak, I think it was – so that she'd think she'd got the better of me. Then Gads came along throwing his bent spears all over the place and nearly messed it up . . ."

Herbert (now visible again) could be heard saying, "And I lifted Demelza up and twirled her around. I'm stronger than I look, you know. You should have seen me – well, you know what I mean."

Sir Gadabout was saying, "It was a lucky shot but I knew that if I aimed at an angle of 47 degrees with a head wind of 3.5 knots, I could just get the hem of Morag's dress."

And Sidney Smith was simply saying, "It was a lucky shot."

If everyone knew deep down that Sir Gadabout was still the Worst Knight in the World, it was quite a while before they mentioned it again.